Phew, Sidney!

The Sweetest-Smelling Skunk in the World!

Rose Impey
Shoo Rayner

ORCHARD BOOKS

ORCHARD BOOKS
96 Leonard Street, London EC2A 4XD
Orchard Books Australia
Unit 31/56 O'Riordan Street, Alexandria, NSW 2015
First published in Great Britain in 1994
This edition published in hardback in 2002
This edition published in paperback in 2003
Text © Rose Impey 1994
Illustrations © Shoo Rayner 2002
The rights of Rose Impey to be identified as the author
and Shoo Rayner as the illustrator of this work
have been asserted by them in accordance with the
Copyright, Designs and Patents Act, 1988.
A CIP catalogue record for this book is
available from the British Library.
ISBN 1 84121 872 3 (hardback)
ISBN 1 84121 234 2 (paperback)
1 3 5 7 9 10 8 6 4 2 (hardback)
1 3 5 7 9 10 8 6 4 2 (paperback)
Printed in Hong Kong.

Phew, Sidney!

All animals smell.
All people smell, for that matter.
Some smell stronger
than others!
But the smelliest animals
in the world are skunks.
Skunks *really* smell!

But Sidney was different.
He didn't smell
like other skunks.
Sidney smelt...sweet.
He was probably
the sweetest smelling skunk
in the world.

Sidney smelt as sweet as
rose petals
and spring mornings

and newly-bathed babies

and freshly-ironed clothes.

Sidney would have smelt
lovely – to you or me.
But to other skunks
Sidney smelt *different*.

He couldn't help it.
It's just the way he was.

When Sidney was little
the other young skunks
held their noses
if they saw him coming.

When Sidney got older
no one wanted to
sit by him at school.

When Sidney was a teenager
none of the girl skunks
wanted to go out with him.

Sidney didn't know what to do.
He tried everything.
First of all Sidney tried
not having a wash.

He tried *not* brushing his fur.

He tried running fast
until he was really sweaty
and then *not* having a shower.

But Sidney still smelt different.

Sidney tried *not* changing his bedclothes – for six months!

He tried
rolling in mud

and mouldy leaves

and rotten fish

TOO
CENSORED
HORRID

and other
horrid things.

The smell soon wore off
and Sidney smelt as *sweet* as ever.

It was the kind of smell
that only a skunk mother
could love.
"Oh, dear," said his mum.
"At this rate, Sidney will be left
on the shelf."
"Not if I can help it,"
said his dad.

So Sidney set off
to see a bit of the world.

Sidney travelled a long way.
He was tired and dusty
and very hungry.
At last he came to a town.
In the middle of the town
there was a big fair.

At the fair there were
all kinds of skunks.

Old skunks and young skunks.

Rich skunks and poor skunks.

Rough skunks and tough skunks.

There were even punk skunks.

But wherever Sidney went
everyone stared at him.
They sniffed the air.
They pulled faces.
They turned away.
So Sidney kept on walking.

Sidney was hungry.
He had to find something to eat.
Sidney found a van
selling hot dogs.

A young girl skunk was serving.
She said, "Hello, handsome."
Sidney was so surprised
he couldn't speak.

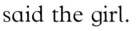

"Cat got your tongue?"
said the girl.

She smiled at Sidney.
She had a lovely smile.

Sidney turned red.

The girl smiled again.
"I think you're shy," she said.
It was true.
Sidney blushed even more.
At last Sidney said,
"Can I have a hot dog?"
"Anything for you,"
said the girl.

Sidney couldn't believe it.
Girls didn't usually talk
to *him* like that.
They usually said,
"Phew, Sidney.
You smell…terrible."
But this girl didn't seem
to notice.
She was so used to the smell
of hot dogs and onions
she couldn't smell anything else.

Sidney watched her frying onions.
She was very good at it.
"What's your name?" Sidney asked.
"Susie," said the girl.

This time *she* blushed.
"That's a nice name," said Sidney.
"I bet you say that to all
the girls," said Susie.
"Oh, no, I don't," said Sidney.
And that was true too.

Susie gave Sidney his hot dog.
She smiled at him.
It was love at first...bite!

So Sidney stayed with the fair.
Wherever Susie's hot dog van went,
Sidney followed.

He helped Susie make hot dogs.
He helped her fry the onions.

After a while he began to smell
of hot dogs and onions too.
The other fairground skunks
soon got used to Sidney.
He was very popular.

Sidney was good with his paws.
He was good at mending things.

He was good at inventing things.

He invented new fairground rides.
He was full of ideas.

His ideas made lots of money.

After a while the other skunks
asked Sidney to run the fair.
Now it was called:
Sidney Skunk's
Super-Dooper Fun Fair.

He and Susie became very rich.
They had lots of baby skunks.
They all smelled of hot dogs
and onions.
They all looked like Sidney –
or Susie.

One day the fair arrived
in a new town.
In fact it was Sidney's *old* town.

When Sidney's friends and family
saw him they were so surprised.
Sidney was such a success.

It was funny that this time
no one mentioned the fact
that Sidney smelt *different*.
Everyone wanted to talk about
how much they used to like Sidney.
What a good friend he had been.
What a super skunk he was.

Sidney still smelt different
but now they all thought,
"What a wonderful smell."
Now they thought,
"It's much better to be different."
They wanted Sidney to settle down
in their town again.

But Sidney said, "No, thanks."
Because Sidney really *was* different.
He wanted a more exciting life.
He liked meeting lots of
different skunks.

He liked seeing different places.
He liked his life on the road.
And so did Susie.
They were both different –
but they were two of a kind.

Crack-A-Joke

What did the skunk say when the wind changed?
It's all coming back to me now!

What smells worse than a skunk?
Two skunks!

What do you call a skunk with a banana in one ear, a sponge finger in the other ear and a jelly on its head?
A trifle smelly!

Jokes not to be sniffed at!

What do you get if you cross
a skunk with a limpet?
A smell you can't get rid of!

What do you get if
you cross a skunk
with an elephant?
**A smell you'll
never forget!**

How does a skunk with
no nose smell?

Absolutely
terrible!

There are 16 Colour Crackers books.
Collect them all!

Colour Crackers are available from all good bookshops,
or can be ordered direct from the publisher:
Orchard Books, PO BOX 29, Douglas IM99 1BQ
Credit card orders please telephone 01624 836000 or fax 01624 837033
or e-mail: bookshop@enterprise.net for details.
To order please quote title, author and ISBN and your full name and address.
Cheques and postal orders should be made payable to 'Bookpost plc'.
Postage and packing is FREE within the UK
(overseas customers should add £1.00 per book).
Prices and availability are subject to change.

1 84121 888 X

1 84121 862 6

1 84121 870 7

1 84121 878 2

1 84121 876 6

1 84121 868 5

1 84121 860 X

1 84121 874 X

1 84121 872 3